Double Trouble

By Jenne Simon
Illustrated by AMEET Studio

SCHOLASTIC INC.

ISBN 978-0-545-56667-4

12 11 10 9 8 7 6 5 4 3 2 1 14 15 16 17 18/0

Printed in the U.S.A. 40
First printing, January 2014

One day at Heartlake High . . .
CLUB FAIR TODAY!
Wow! This activity fair is awesome.
There are so many clubs.
I can't decide which one to join.

It looks like Andrea already has.
Hey, girls! I just joined the Heartlake High Chorus.
This is the song director, Mrs. Lee.
We're excited to have Andrea sing with us. Our first concert is next Friday.
Wow! That's great!

In fact, we have a favor to ask you girls.
We need people to work on costumes, lights, and sound.
costumes
lights
sound
You had me at "costumes!"
We're in!
Thanks, girls! We couldn't do it without you.

Stephanie joined her friends as they walked to class.

Guess what, guys. I joined the soccer team. The coach is making me a forward!

Wow—that's amazing, Stephanie!

Thanks! But I'm really nervous. I'm the youngest player on the team. Will you guys come to my first game?
Of course!
We can't wait to cheer you on.
Olivia
You guys are the best! See you later!

After Stephanie left, Andrea noticed something.
Come See the Soccer Team's First Game Next Friday!
Oh, no!

Come See the Soccer Team's First Game Next Friday!
My concert and Stephanie's soccer game are on the same night!

Yikes! What are we going to do?
Let's talk to Mrs. Lee. Maybe only one of us needs to work the concert.
Is it okay if only one of us works the show?
I'm sorry, girls. It's definitely a three-person job. I'm counting on you.
Now what?
We'll have to tell Stephanie. Maybe she'll understand.

Later, Olivia and Mia went to the soccer field.
Hey, Stephanie! Can we talk to you?
Sure! But first, watch this.

Dribbbbble

Score!

As long as you guys are here, I'll play just like that next Friday!

That's just it, Steph. We—
Can't wai
you play! R
We have
bye!
Why didn't you tell her? We can't be in two places at once.
I know, but she was so excited. We'll figure something out.

The next day, at Science Club . . .
Hi, Olivia.
Oh, hi, Jacob.
I'm fixing these walkie-talkies. They work in places cell phones can't.
Oh . . . cool.
Is something wrong?
Stephanie wants us at her game next Friday. But we promised to work Andrea's concert that night.

Olivia and Jacob test the walkie-talkies.
Stephanie must be pretty bummed.
We haven't told her yet.
You haven't? Why not?
She was so excited. I didn't want to disappoint her.

Won't she be more hurt if you can't come *and* you didn't tell her?
I guess you're right.

Later, the girls did homework together.
Stephanie, we need to tell you something.
What's up?
We can't come to your game.
But why? You promised!
We already signed up to work Andrea's concert.
You're going to Andrea's concert, but not my game?

We didn't know they were the same night. We're so sorry, Steph.
I can't believe you guys won't be there. I-I've got to go.
I feel terrible.
This is all my fault. I shouldn't have asked you guys to help with my concert.

You didn't know. If only there was a way to see Stephanie's game at the same time.
HIGH SCHOOL
Wait a minute. What about our smartphones? Olivia, do you think Jacob would stream us video of Stephanie's game?
That's a great idea! Let's go ask him.

At the auditorium . . .
I'd love to help, girls, but there's no cell service in here.
I guess there really *isn't* anything we can do.
Don't be so sure.
Jacob, can you think of anything that works where cell phones can't?
Olivia, you're a genius!

The following Friday, at the concert . . .
Thank you so much, guys. I really appreciate your help!
Anytime! And, Olivia, is your plan ready?
Just about. Jacob? Come in, Jacob. Can you hear me?

Over on the soccer field . . .
Do you read me, Jacob?
Loud and clear, Olivia!

How are you doing, Stephanie?
I'm really nervous. I wish the others were here, too.

Just wait. I think they might surprise you.

The concert and soccer game were both about to begin.

All right, Jacob. Here we go!

Everything's ready, Olivia!

Here's to our dear
Heartlake High...
All that practice really paid off. The chorus sounds amazing!

During the intermission, the girls focused on the soccer game.
Stephanie's shooting for the goal. Oh, she just missed!
Come on, Stephanie. We know you can do it!

Back on the field . . .
Good try, Stephanie!
Thanks, Jacob. But I'm not doing very well.
That's not true. We know you're doing great!
Olivia? Emma? Mia? Is that you?

I think Stephanie's figured out the surprise.
We're here for you, Stephanie!
You guys did this for me? You're the best! Now watch—I mean, *listen* to this!
Stephanie stole the ball from the other team!
You can do it, Stephanie! Go for the goal!

Just then, the concert intermission ended.
It's almost time for Andrea's solo, Jacob. But we'll have the walkie-talkie right here.
Sounds good. I'll keep you posted on Steph's game!

The friends watched Andrea sing her solo onstage.
We can do it, if you just believe!
Her voice is magical!

A short while later . . .
Brava, Andrea! That was an amazing concert.
Guys, is it finished? Hurry over here! The game is going into overtime!
We can still make it!
Let's go!

We're coming, Stephanie!
Jacob, we're on our way!
All right!
The girls arrived at the field just in time.
Did we make it? Is it over?
Nope. Look—there goes Stephanie!

She's got the ball.
2:2
2:2
And there's only a minute left!
Kick!
Hurray!
Goal for Heartlake High!

I can't believe you guys heard the whole game!
Jacob gave us an awesome play-by-play. It was like we were right here on the sidelines.

It was all thanks to Olivia's idea.
We knew how much it meant to you.

Thank you so much. I don't know what I'd do without you guys.
That goes double for me!